Who framed ROGER RABBIT™

Make the World Laugh

Based on the motion picture from
Walt Disney Pictures and Steven Spielberg

Executive Producers
STEVEN SPIELBERG   KATHLEEN KENNEDY   FRANK MARSHALL
Produced by
ROBERT WATTS
Screenplay by
JEFFREY PRICE & PETER SEAMAN
Directed by
ROBERT ZEMECKIS
Storybook adapted by
JUSTINE KORMAN
Illustrated by
AL WHITE STUDIOS

A GOLDEN BOOK • NEW YORK

Western Publishing Company, Inc., Racine, Wisconsin 53404

Eddie Valiant was the world's gloomiest detective. He hadn't laughed in ten years, and he hadn't had a case in almost as long. Eddie sat in his dingy office with his feet up on his dingy desk.

Suddenly there was a knock at the door. When Eddie opened it, he saw a goofy-looking Toon rabbit, ears quivering and knees knocking with fear.

"You've got to help me!" Roger Rabbit exclaimed. Eddie slammed the door in Roger's face.

"I don't work for Toons," Eddie growled through the door.

"Why not?" Roger asked from his comfortable spot in Eddie's chair.

"Huh? How did you—" the detective stammered.

"I slipped in through the mail slot," Roger explained. "Please, you must help me. The Toon Patrol is after me. But I'm innocent!"

There was another knock at the door.
Eddie threw Roger into the sink with the socks he was soaking.

"Stay under the bubbles," Valiant commanded.
Then he opened the door for the weasel Toon Patrol.

"We're looking for a rabbit," the chief weasel said.

"Try a carrot patch," Eddie replied.

"He's a dangerous fugitive, and we have reason to believe he came to you for help," the weasel added.

"I don't help Toons," Eddie snapped, and he slammed the door.

When the weasels were gone, Roger floated out
of the sink in a giant bubble and planted a soapy
Toon kiss on Eddie's cheek.

"Thanks! I knew you'd help!" Roger said
gratefully.

"Get out," Eddie replied. "I didn't help them,
and I won't help you."

"I can pay you lots of money," Roger offered.

Eddie hesitated, then shook Roger's paw.

"You can hide at the Terminal Café," Eddie said, grabbing his coat. "My girlfriend, Dolores, is a waitress there."

Eddie hid Roger under his coat and went to the café. But Roger was a curious Toon, and he kept popping out from inside Eddie's coat. Dolores looked at Eddie and Roger and said, "I've heard of pulling a rabbit out of a hat—but out of a coat?"

"This is serious, Dolores," said Eddie. "The Toon Patrol is after this rabbit, and he needs to hide in the back room until I can figure out who really committed the crime."

Dolores agreed to help Roger.

"Now, don't make a sound," Eddie instructed the rabbit. "And don't open the door to anyone, except me or Dolores."

Roger nodded dutifully, and Eddie and Dolores left the café to do some investigating.

But it wasn't long before Roger felt restless. Through the peephole, he could see the Terminal's regular customers staring into space or picking sadly at plates of tired french fries and soggy eggs.

"They need me!" Roger thought, and his ears perked up and his eyes brightened. Roger's reason for being was to make the world laugh.

Roger burst out of his hiding place and began entertaining the customers with songs and jokes. Soon all the oddball regulars were having a great time, singing along with Roger's funny songs and joining in his zany antics.

The old cowboy laughed himself right off his stool when the rabbit gave him an exploding cigar. And no one had ever seen big, tough Angelo laugh, until Roger shook his hand with his favorite trick, the hand buzzer.

Then Eddie came back, and the fun was over.

"How could you be so stupid?" Eddie
demanded as he rushed Roger back into his
hiding place. "Those characters would turn you
in for a dime!"

But Roger didn't think so. He liked his new
friends. He had made them laugh and was
certain they would not betray him.

"Shh!" Eddie hissed, and he peeped through the peephole. It was Judge Doom and his weasel Toon Patrol!

"Which one of you would like $5,000?" Doom asked as he and his weasels swarmed into the café.

The Terminal regulars murmured excitedly.

"Just tell me where I can find Roger Rabbit," Doom boomed, "and the reward money is yours."

Roger waited tensely as silence fell over the room.

"Roger Rabbit," Angelo said. "White fur, long ears, goofy expression. Yeah, I've seen him."

"Where?" Doom demanded.

"In the movies," Angelo replied, and everyone in the room burst out laughing.

Eddie was amazed. Roger beamed. "See?" he
told Eddie. "I knew they wouldn't let me down."
"What's this?" Doom thundered, and he held
up Roger's hand buzzer for all to see.

"That rabbit is here!" Judge Doom declared.
"And I'll get him yet!"
  Doom knocked on the countertop, on the
walls, and on the floor. He knocked in a special
rhythm irresistible to all Toons: Da da-da-da-da!
"Shave and a haircut…"

Roger couldn't help himself. He burst from the back room and shouted the end of the jingle: "Two bits!"

He was quickly grabbed by Doom's weasels.

"Now to Dip this troublesome rabbit!" Judge Doom gloated, pulling Roger toward a vat of vile-smelling liquid.

"Not the Dip!" Roger begged miserably.

"What's the Dip?" Angelo asked.

"The only thing that can get rid of a Toon," Doom explained. "Turpentine, benzine, and a dash of bitters...makes them disappear forever!"

Roger tried everything he could to escape the
Dip. One desperate paw found a bottle of
ketchup, and Roger bashed it over a weasel's
head with a loud POP!

"Pop goes the weasel," Eddie said. And then an
amazing thing happened.

A laugh bubbled up from his toes to his nose.
It grew and grew until it was a laugh big enough
for ten laughless years. And it spread from Eddie
to Dolores, to the Terminal regulars, and even to
Doom's weasels, who were soon so convulsed
with giggles, they could only watch helplessly as
Eddie and Roger ran out the door.

"After them!" Doom commanded.
But the weasels only laughed harder.

Outside, Benny, a jazzy Toon roadster, offered
Eddie and Roger a lift. As they sped away from
Doom and his weasels, Eddie Valiant felt better
than he had in years.

"You can keep your money," the detective told
his funny new friend. "That laugh was worth a
million bucks."